HOPSCOTCH ADVENTURES

The Dragon and the Pudding

by Martin Remphry

D0993812

First published in 2009 by
Franklin Watts
338 Euston Road
London
NW1 3BH

Franklin Watts Australia
Level 17/207 Kent Street
Sydney
NSW 2000

Text and Illustrations © Martin Remphry 2009

The right of Martin Remphry to be identified as the author
and illustrator of this Work has been asserted in accordance
with the Copyright, Designs and Patents Act, 1988.

All rights reserved. No part of this publication may be
reproduced, stored in a retrieval system, or transmitted
in any form or by any means, electronic, mechanical,
photocopy, recording or otherwise, without the prior
written permission of the copyright owner.

A CIP catalogue record for this book is available
from the British Library.

ISBN 978 0 7496 8549 2 (hbk)
ISBN 978 0 7496 8561 4 (pbk)

Series Editor: Jackie Hamley
Series Advisor: Dr Barrie Wade
Series Designer: Peter Scoulding

Printed in China

Franklin Watts is a division of
Hachette Children's Books,
an Hachette UK company
www.hachette.co.uk

**For Leon – who loves
dragons and pudding!**

Long ago in Lyminster there was
a horrible dragon. He was called
Knucker, and he lived in a deep
pond near the village.

Knucker ate all the animals.
When he ran out of them, he
licked people off the road and
gobbled them up, just like a
toad licking up flies.

The mayor knew that Knucker
had to be stopped.

So she offered a bag of gold to anyone who could get rid of him.

REWARD

A BAG OF GOLD TO GET RID OF KNUCKER

But the villagers were too scared
to go near Knucker's pond.

Then, one day, a boy called Jim
who lived in the village of Wick,
not far away, came to Lyminster.

"I have heard about your dragon,
and I can get rid of him!"
said Jim to the mayor.
"But you are just a boy!"
replied the mayor.

"I may be a boy, and I may need some help, but I can get rid of Knucker!" Jim promised.

11

The mayor told the villagers
to give Jim whatever he needed.
First, Jim went to the blacksmith.
"I need your biggest pot," he said.

Next, he went to the miller.

"I need all your flour," he said.

Then Jim gathered the villagers together. "I need you all to make a huge fire in the Square!" he told them.

Jim beat the flour with water and
mixed a huge pudding in the pot.

16

Then all the people lifted it onto
the enormous fire. It was the
stickiest, heaviest pudding
anyone had ever seen.

Next day, the pudding was ready. Everybody helped Jim to lift it onto some logs and roll it down the hill.

When they reached Knucker's pond, the villagers became scared.

Knucker's head was sticking out of the water, and his tail lay up the hill, knocking over trees in the next village.

Soon Jim was left alone with
the enormous pudding and
the horrible dragon.
"What's that?" roared the dragon.

22

"Pudding," replied Jim.

"Well I shall eat it first and then I shall eat you," thundered the dragon, lumbering out of the pond.

Jim hid behind a tree as Knucker
gulped down the pudding and the
logs with it.

He waited until he heard Knucker
give a terrible moan.

"What's wrong, dragon?" yelled Jim.
"My stomach hurts!" roared
Knucker. "I can't move!"

"Let me help then," cried Jim.
But instead he raced up and
cut off the dragon's head.

"Hurrah for Jim!" cheered the villagers. Later Jim shared the gold to thank them for their help.

Knucker's pond is still near Lyminster, but no dragons live in it now. At least, we don't think so ...

Puzzle 1

Put these pictures in the correct order.
Which event do you think is most important?
Now try writing the story in your own words!

Puzzle 2

1. I'll eat you all for supper!

2. What can his plan be?

3. I'll need a big pot!

4. I can get rid of your dragon.

5. I don't like pudding any more!

6. Here's a bag of gold to get rid of Knucker!

Choose the correct speech bubbles for each character. Can you think of any others? Turn over to find the answers.

Answers

Puzzle 1

The correct order is: 1a, 2f, 3c, 4b, 5e, 6d

Puzzle 2

Knucker: 1, 5

Jim: 3, 4

The mayor: 2, 6

Look out for more Hopscotch Adventures:

Aladdin and the Lamp
ISBN 978 0 7496 6692 7

Blackbeard the Pirate
ISBN 978 0 7496 6690 3

George and the Dragon
ISBN 978 0 7496 6691 0

Jack the Giant-Killer
ISBN 978 0 7496 6693 4

Beowulf and Grendel
ISBN 978 0 7496 8551 5*
ISBN 978 0 7496 8563 8

Agnes and the Giant
ISBN 978 0 7496 8552 2*
ISBN 978 0 7496 8564 5

The Dragon and the Pudding
ISBN 978 0 7496 8549 2*
ISBN 978 0 7496 8561 4

Finn MacCool and the Giant's Causeway
ISBN 978 0 7496 8550 8*
ISBN 978 0 7496 8562 1

TALES OF KING ARTHUR

1. The Sword in the Stone
ISBN 978 0 7496 6694 1

2. Arthur the King
ISBN 978 0 7496 6695 8

3. The Round Table
ISBN 978 0 7496 6697 2

4. Sir Lancelot and the Ice Castle
ISBN 978 0 7496 6698 9

5. Sir Gawain and the Green Knight
ISBN 978 0 7496 8557 7*
ISBN 978 0 7496 8569 0

6. Sir Galahad and the Holy Grail
ISBN 978 0 7496 8558 4*
ISBN 978 0 7496 8570 6

TALES OF ROBIN HOOD

Robin and the Knight
ISBN 978 0 7496 6699 6

Robin and the Monk
ISBN 978 0 7496 6700 9

Robin and the Silver Arrow
ISBN 978 0 7496 6703 0

Robin and the Friar
ISBN 978 0 7496 6702 3

Robin and the Butcher
ISBN 978 0 7496 8555 3*
ISBN 978 0 7496 8568 3

Robin and Maid Marian
ISBN 978 0 7496 8556 0*
ISBN 978 0 7496 8567 6

For more Hopscotch books go to:
www.franklinwatts.co.uk

* hardback   **Tales of Sinbad the Sailor also available!**